KU-350-910

Contents

First published 2018 by Brown Watson
The Old Mill, 76 Fleckney Road
Kibworth Beauchamp
Leicestershire LE8 0HG

ISBN: 978 0 7097 2613 5

Printed in Malaysia

Brown Watson
ENGLAND

Danny's First Day

Danny the dinosaur is lost. His family has just arrived here, and he doesn't know his way around. It all seems very strange.

'Hello!' trumpets a purple dinosaur. 'I'm Penny. What's your name? Are you new here? I can show you around, if you like?'

Danny swallows nervously. 'I would love that, thank you. My name is Danny. This is my first day here.'

Penny whistles loudly and more dinosaurs appear. 'Hey, guys! Say hi to Danny. I've promised that we will give him a tour.'

First, they show him the mighty waterfall. 'We come here every morning for a shower,' they explain.

Next, they show him the woods. ‘We play hide and seek here,’ they say. ‘But only at the edge. We’re not allowed too far into the trees.’

There is just one place left for Danny to see. They have saved the best until last. 'Close your eyes and let us guide you,' they say.

'WOW!' gasps Danny. 'What is it?'
'It's a volcano!' they all say, proudly.
'Do you like it?'
'I LOVE it!' says Danny, and lets out a happy roar.

Happy Birthday!

Daisy can hear a croaking noise coming from the pond. It sounds like singing. She creeps closer to take a look.

It is Freya Frog, singing to herself. ‘Happy birthday to me! Happy birthday to me! Happy birthday, little Freya, happy birthday to me!’

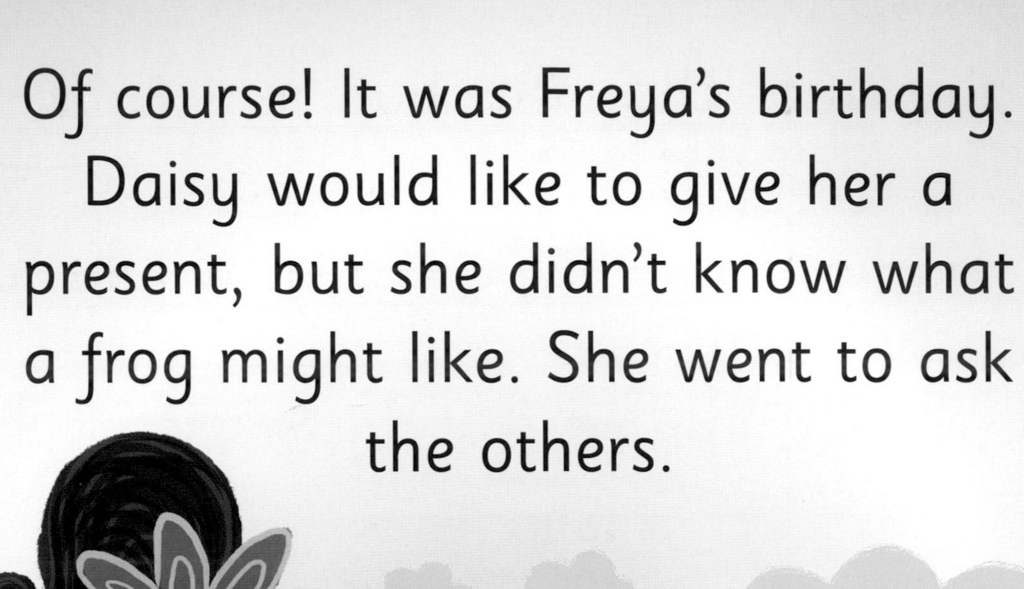

Of course! It was Freya's birthday. Daisy would like to give her a present, but she didn't know what a frog might like. She went to ask the others.

Baby Duck thought that Freya might like a crown. Then she would look like a frog princess! But a crown would fall off when Freya dived and jumped.

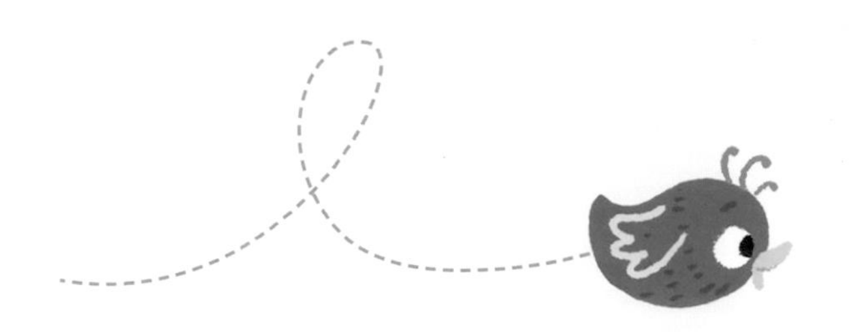

'Mummy,' asked Baby Duck, 'what presents do frogs like?' Mummy thought for a while, and then gave them a great idea.

Daisy and Baby Duck were very busy. They looked around the edge of the pond for the things they needed to make a special gift. They spent a long time, working very carefully to get it just right.

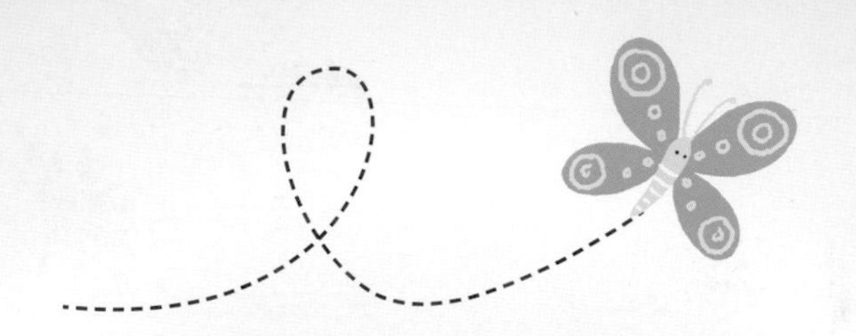

Then they went looking for Freya Frog again. When they found her, they sang as loudly as they could.

'Happy birthday to you, happy birthday to you, we've made you some presents, happy birthday to you!'

Freya was very happy. Now she has a special hand-made necklace from two of her best friends.

Runaway

'Look at the shapes in the clouds,' says Daddy. 'What can you see?'

'I can see a bike, and a mushroom!' says Maddie.

'I can see a dog like Rusty,' says Daddy. Rusty gives a little bark. 'And I can see a sheep.'

Daddy falls asleep in the sunshine. Maddie and Rusty decide to explore the field around them. As they walk around the edge, Maddie can hear some real sheep.

'Baa! Baa!' say the sheep. Rusty's ears prick up. He runs to look into the next field. Maddie catches up, and peeps over as well. There they are!

Maddie smiles as the baby lambs leap around. Then she gasps. Rusty has jumped over the hedge. 'Rusty, no!' she shouts.

Maddie is afraid that Rusty will frighten the sheep. But Rusty isn't being naughty. He has seen a runaway sheep, escaping into the next field.

Maddie watches as Rusty runs into the field. He hurries past the sheep and stands in front of it. The sheep stops, and turns around. Rusty creeps towards it, making the sheep run back to join the rest of the flock.

Daddy has joined Maddie and sees what Rusty is doing. 'Well done, boy!' smiles Daddy. 'What a good dog you are!'

Finding Friends

'Come with me,' says Molly. She grabs her friend Alice by the hand. 'The princess is sad and we need to help her.'

Alice has to run to keep up with Molly. Molly runs fast, even though she is only small! They make their way to the garden behind the palace. They can hear Princess Jenna crying.

'All of my friends have gone back to school,' she sniffs, 'but I am still too young for school. I have nobody to play with. Even you two are going away and leaving me!'

Molly and Alice give Princess Jenna a big hug. 'Leave it with us,' they promise. 'We won't let you be lonely while we are away.'

Molly dashes off. She calls out to Squirrel who is gathering food. 'Please will you help to look after the princess?'

Alice tiptoes up to Rabbit and asks for her help. Rabbit is more than happy to be Princess Jenna's friend.

Then Deer trots past and asks what is happening. When she hears the problem, she says that she will help too.

'Can we be the princess's friends?' asks Hedgehog and Mouse. 'Of course!' replies Alice. 'That would be lovely.'

Molly and Alice meet again in the back garden. They skip up to Princess Jenna. 'Look how many new friends we have found for you,' they say. All of the animals gather around.

The Princess can't believe her eyes. 'And will you really come to play when everyone else is away?' she asks. The thought of it makes her very happy indeed.

Telling the Truth

Mummy was getting ready to collect her children from school. She changed out of her work clothes and brushed her hair. Then she looked out of the window.

What a mess! Her lovely flowerpot was broken and there was dirt everywhere. She stomped off to school to find out how her children had broken it.

Mummy met Bobby and Fran in the classroom. 'My garden is such a mess!' she complained. 'I need you to help me tidy it as soon as we get home.'

But when they arrived home, Bobby and Fran were as shocked as Mummy had been. 'I didn't do it!' said Bobby. 'And I didn't do it!' said Fran.

‘Well, if you didn’t do it, how did it happen?’ asked Mummy. Then the doorbell rang. A little girl stood outside.

‘Please can I have my ball back?’ she asked. ‘My friend kicked it over your wall this morning. I hope it didn’t do any damage. We’re very sorry if it did.’

Mummy smiled and asked Bobby and Fran to collect the ball. She handed it to the little girl. 'Be more careful from now on,' she said.

'Aren't you cross anymore?' asked Fran. Mummy gave them a cuddle. 'Not at all,' she said. 'Accidents happen. And I am glad that you were both telling me the truth all along.'

Little Lost Lion

Leroy woke up from his afternoon sleep. He stretched and yawned and stood up. His mummy was still asleep in the shade.

Leroy heard a noise and looked up. It was a pretty butterfly, flying past Leroy's ears. He wondered where it was going.

'Oh, hello Ossie!' said Leroy. 'Don't worry, I won't stand on your eggs. I am just following the butterfly.'

Leroy padded on. 'Oh, hello Zoey!' he said. 'Look at the pretty butterfly! Do you want to follow it with me?'

But Zoey wanted to stay in the cool grass.

Leroy skipped on his way. 'Hi, Jilly,' he shouted up into the trees. 'Look at the pretty butterfly!'

But the butterfly had flown away. Now Leroy was far from home, and frightened. 'Don't worry,' said Jilly. 'I can see your mummy from here.'

Jilly showed Leroy which way he should run. He set off as fast as he could. Before long, he could hear roaring. 'Mummy, mummy! I'm here,' he shouted.

Mummy was very pleased to see him. Leroy was even more pleased to see her! He snuggled into her soft warm fur for a cuddle. He wouldn't be chasing butterflies again for a long time.

Princess Betsy

Princess Betsy loves her daddy so much. He may be very important, but he always spends time with his beloved daughter.

He wakes her up every morning and opens her curtains so they can see if it is sunny or raining. They have lunch together and sometimes they eat their sandwiches sitting on his throne! Her daddy sits with Betsy every day and teaches her to read.

The king shows Betsy how to clean her teeth and fold her clothes neatly. He teaches her to dance, and they twirl around her room together as if they are at a royal ball.

Each night, the king sneaks away from his important dinner guests so that he can read Betsy a story. He tucks her into bed and kisses her goodnight. Then he turns out the light and goes back to being king.

One day, the king has some sad news.
He has to go on a royal trip, and
he cannot take Betsy with him.
She will miss him so much.

The king promises to talk to Betsy every day. He will use his fancy phone to see and speak to her and even read her a bedtime story. He promises he will be back as soon as he can.

The king has another piece of news for Betsy. He doesn't want her to be too sad or lonely while he is away, so he has bought her a present.

'Hey, Prince!' he whistles, and a puppy bounds into the room. 'I command you to look after my daughter for me, and to stay by her side at all times!'
Betsy is delighted!

Secret Hideaway

'Ouch!' Jamie was lying in the woods, daydreaming, when something hard hit him on the head. 'What was that?' he said to himself. Then another one hit him, and he picked it up. It was an acorn.

'It's the bears,' squeaked a tiny voice in his ear. 'The bears are playing naughty tricks.'

Jamie began to think he was dreaming. A little squirrel stood by his side, telling him that there were bears in the trees. And they were throwing acorns at everyone!

Jamie wasn't happy about it. He thought they should find a way to stop those naughty bears. He whispered his idea to the squirrel, who nodded eagerly.

Jamie crept to the bottom of the bears' tree, as quietly as he could. The squirrel showed him a way inside, and then scampered silently up the trunk, as quick as a flash.

Jamie waited inside the hollow trunk until he heard a rumble and a bump. The squirrel had put their plan into action!

Jamie chuckled to himself as the squirrel began to roll acorns down the stairs.

Jamie gathered them all up until his pockets were full, and then took them to the squirrel's secret hiding place. Now the bears would have nothing to throw, and the squirrel would have food for the whole of winter!

Around the World

The children are excited. It is their geography lesson with Miss Fielding, and her classes are always fun. 'Good morning, class!' she says. 'Today I am wearing clothes from somewhere very hot. Can anyone tell me some hot places?'

Alfie shouts out, 'The desert, Miss!' and she congratulates him. Then she tells them all to close their eyes and hold hands tightly.

1 × 2 =
2 × 3 =
3 × 2 =

With a whoosh and a flash, the children are whisked away to explore the desert for themselves. Miss Fielding guides them through the sandy dunes and shows them how people live in such a hot, dry land.

They all groan when she says it is time to go home. She quickly counts up to make sure no one gets left behind. That would be a disaster!

‘What are you wearing today, Miss Fielding?’ her pupils ask. She tells them that her trousers are from India, where it also gets very hot.

The class close their eyes and hold hands again. This time, they find themselves in some beautiful palace gardens. It has fountains to keep them cool. 'Wow!' gasps Tilly.

The Headmistress comes into Friday's geography lesson. 'Congratulations!' she says. 'You have been voted the number 1 teacher! Could you come to my office to collect your award?'

Miss Fielding smiles proudly, but explains that she will be a little late. 'First of all, we have to learn about the Stars and Stripes flag,' she explains. The children clap and cheer. 'Woohoo! America here we come!'